USBORNE HOTSHOTS

CREEPY CRAWLIES

USBORNE HOTSHOTS

CREEPY CRAWLIES

Edited by Mandy Ross

Designed by Karen Tomlins

Illustrated by Chris Shields, Phil Weare, Ian Jackson and Doreen McGuinness

Series editor: Judy Tatchell

Series designer: Ruth Russell

Consultant: Margaret Rostron

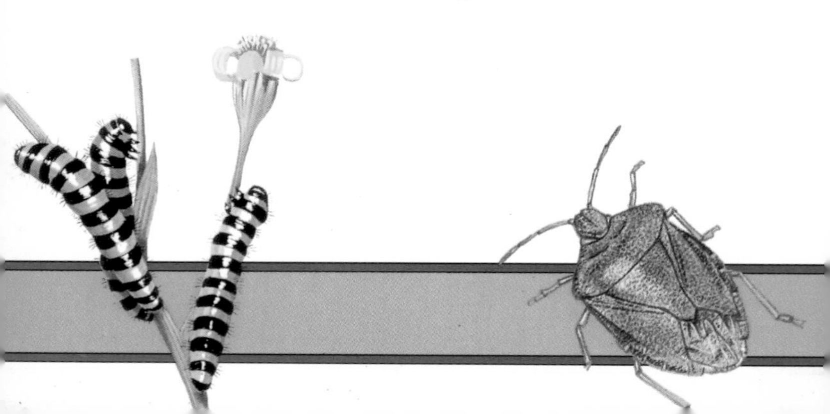

CONTENTS

How to use this book

This book shows some of the millions of creepy crawlies on our planet. Many are familiar types, or species, who live in or around your home. Others are rare, strange and spectacular. How many can you spot and record on the scorecard on pages 30-31?

Most creepy crawlies are shown bigger than life-size. The number in the magnifying glass gives an idea of how many times bigger. If there is no magnifying glass, the picture is life-size.

When to look

The best time to look for creepy crawlies is in spring, summer and autumn. They are usually more active in warmer weather. Most species in this book can be found across Europe and North America. A few are included which live only in the warmer climates of southern Europe or the southern states of the USA.

Spotting and identifying

When you spot a creepy crawly, try to count its legs, wings and body-parts. Its patterns or markings will also help to identify it.

Two feelers called antennae

Three-part body: head thorax abdomen

Three pairs of legs are joined to the thorax.

Most insects have wings at some stage in their lives.

Insects

All insects have three body parts and six legs, like this wasp. Insects are shown on pages 6-22.

Not insects

The rest of the creepy crawlies in this book (pages 23-27) are not insects.

Spiders have eight legs, and never have wings.

Slugs, snails and worms move without legs.

Millipedes, centipedes and woodlice have many legs. Their bodies have lots of parts, called segments.

Growing and changing

All insects change shape as they grow to adulthood. There are two main ways of changing.

Butterflies, beetles, bees and flies go through the four stages shown below.

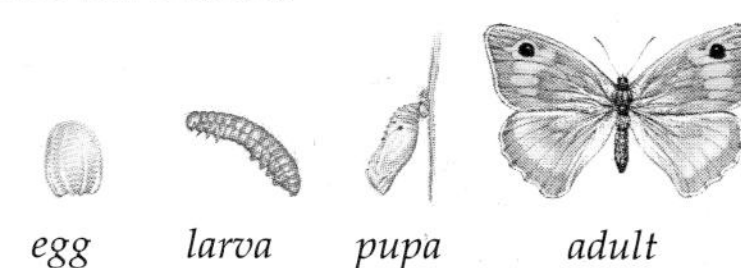

*A **larva** (plural: larvae) is a soft-bodied grub which will turn into a pupa (or chrysalis) before it reaches adulthood.*

Grasshoppers, crickets, bugs and dragonflies develop in a different way. They hatch from eggs as nymphs.

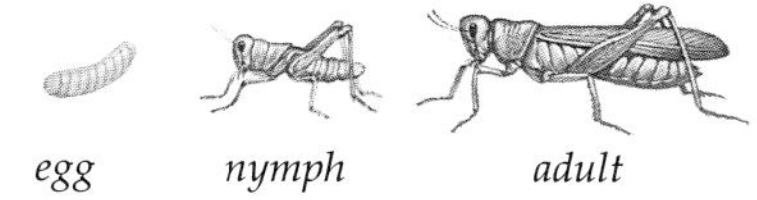

*A **nymph** is a smaller form of the adult, but without wings. It sheds its skin as it grows, but never becomes a pupa.*

Other creepy crawlies who are not insects (like snails and spiders) usually hatch from eggs as smaller forms of the adult.

Tiny snails hatch from eggs. Their shells grow as the snails get bigger.

Did you know..?

Insects have extraordinary muscular strength. If they had lungs – instead of tiny breathing tubes running through their bodies – they might have developed into far larger, powerful animals.

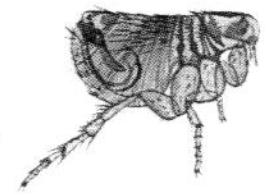

A flea can jump 200 times the length of its own body.

A cockroach can scuttle 12 times its body length in a second. The human equivalent would be running at 65km (40 miles) per hour. The fastest human athletes can sprint at about 36km (22 miles) per hour.

There are over a million species of insects – more than all the other animal species combined. One in three insects is a beetle.

A thread of spider's silk is stronger than a steel wire of the same thickness.

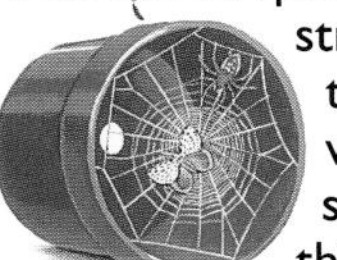

Beetles on land

Beetles are the largest group of insects with about 250,000 known species. They have hard wing cases, called *elytra*, which fold over their wings and abdomen. All beetles bite and chew their food.

Male Stag Beetles use their antlers for fighting and to attract females, just like deer. The larvae live and feed on old tree stumps for three years before they turn into beetles. As adults, they can fly well.

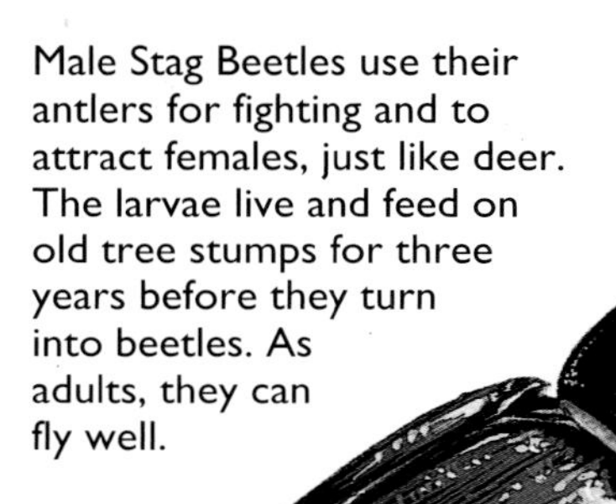

The "antlers" are in fact enlarged jaws.

Stag Beetle

Stag Beetles can grow nearly as big as the one shown here – up to 75mm (3in) long from head to tail.

Ladybirds

Ladybirds and their larvae eat aphids (or greenfly) so gardeners welcome them. There are lots of similar species, with different patterns or numbers of spots. Some species hibernate in large groups through the winter in attics, sheds or tree bark.

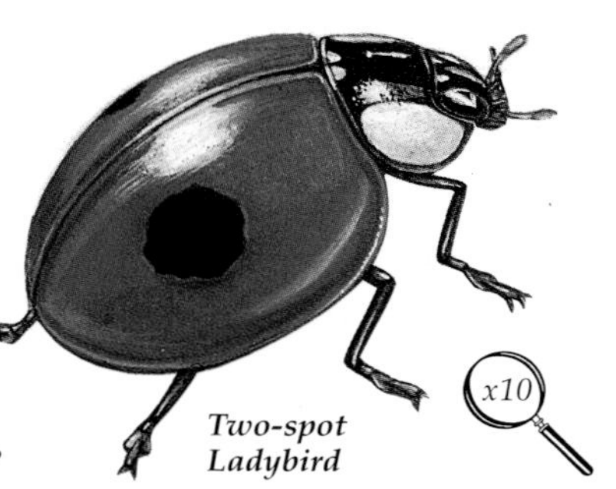

Two-spot Ladybird

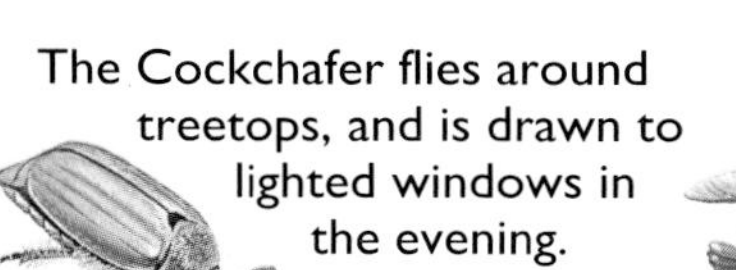

The Cockchafer flies around treetops, and is drawn to lighted windows in the evening.

Like other beetles, the Cockchafer holds up its wing cases, or elytra, in flight.

Cockchafer Beetle

x2

The female Nut Weevil pierces a hazel nut with her rostrum or snout, and lays an egg inside. The larva eats the kernel.

Hazel nut cut away to show larva inside.

Nut Weevil

x2

Colorado Beetle

x2

The Colorado Beetle causes serious damage to potato crops. It was introduced into Europe by accident from America. Tell the police if you spot one.

Turned on its back, the Click Beetle leaps into the air and rights itself with a loud click.

Click Beetle

x3

Here are some more species of ladybirds.

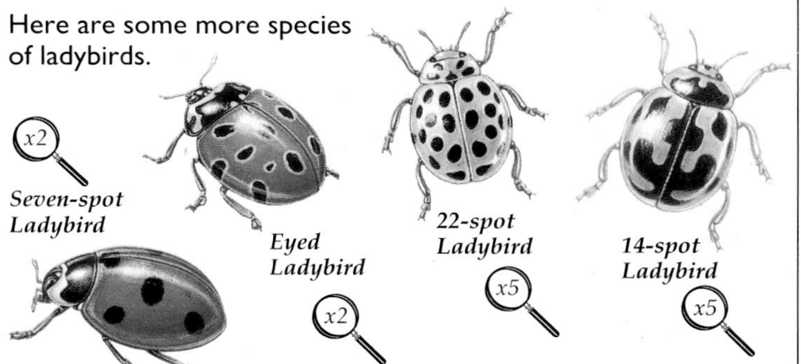

Seven-spot Ladybird *x2*

Eyed Ladybird *x2*

22-spot Ladybird *x5*

14-spot Ladybird *x5*

Predators and scavengers

These beetles are designed for survival in a dangerous world. They use strong jaws, deadly chemicals – and teamwork too.

Green Tiger Beetle x3

The Green Tiger Beetle is a fierce, fast-flying predator, eating ants and other insects. Its larvae are also predators.

To fend off predators, the Bombadier Beetle shoots irritating gas from its abdomen with a popping sound. It is found in warm climates.

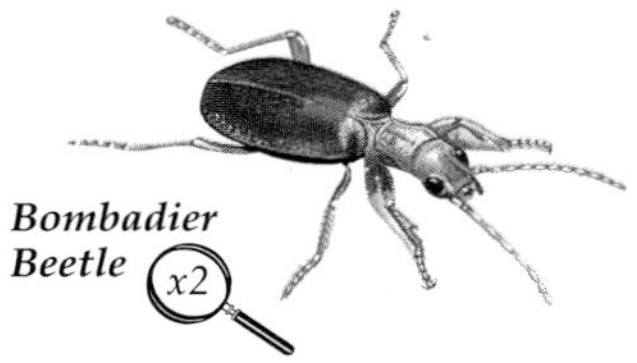

Bombadier Beetle x2

When challenged, a Devil's Coach Horse Beetle raises its tail and oozes poisonous liquid. It hunts by night for larvae, snails and slugs.

Devil's Coach Horse Beetle

Burying Beetles work in pairs to bury dead animal flesh as food for their larvae.

Red and Black Burying Beetle

Hercules Beetle, *shown about half life-size*

The American Hercules Beetle grows to be the longest in the world, at around 190mm (7½in). It is not found in Europe.

Camouflage

Many beetles use markings and patterns to help them fend off predators, blend into their surroundings, or attract a mate. Here are a few of them.

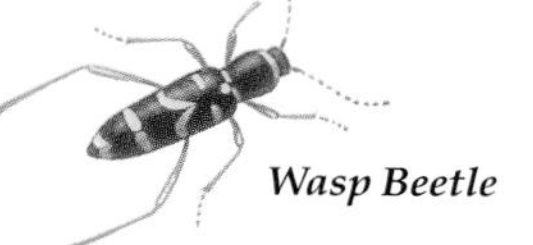

Wasp Beetle

Neither the Wasp Beetle nor the Bee Beetle can sting. But their markings and behaviour mimic stinging insects, to protect them from predators.

Bee Beetle (x2)

Scarlet-tipped Flower Beetle (x2)

The Scarlet-tipped Flower Beetle blows up scarlet bladders on its underside to alarm predators. It is found in warm climates.

Green Tortoise Beetle (x2)

With its legs and antennae hidden, it looks like a tiny tortoise.

The Green Tortoise Beetle is well camouflaged on thistles, where it feeds. It gets its name from its appearance.

Glow-worm

The wingless female Glow-worm, found on grassy hillsides in warmer climates in Europe, attracts a mate with her glowing tail. Fireflies are a similar American species.

Glow-worm (female)

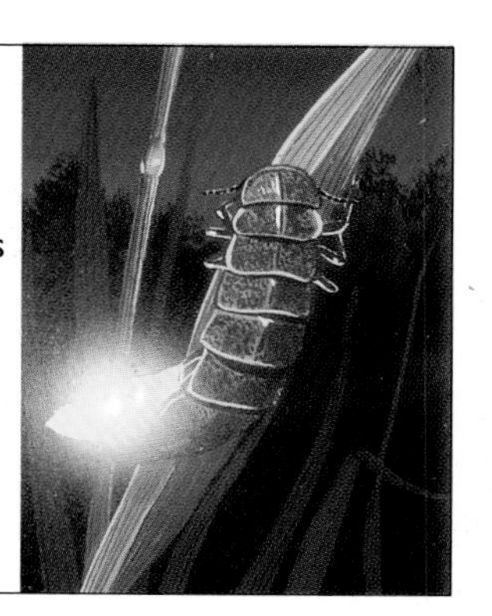

Bugs on land

Unlike beetles, a bug eats by stabbing plants or animal flesh with its tiny needle-like beak or rostrum, and sucking up fluids.

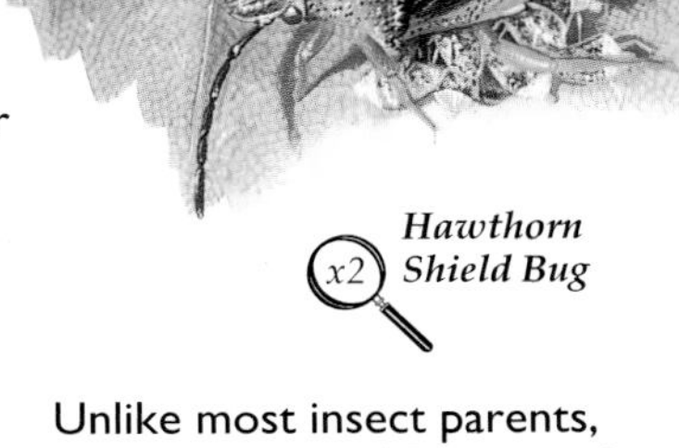

x2 *Hawthorn Shield Bug*

Shield Bugs

Shield Bugs get their name from the shape of their bodies and wings. They are also known as stinkbugs, because they fend off predators with an evil-smelling liquid – which can give humans a headache.

Unlike most insect parents, Hawthorn Shield Bugs stand guard over their eggs and young.

Green Shield Bug x2

The female Green Shield Bug lays batches of eggs on trees like hazel and birch.

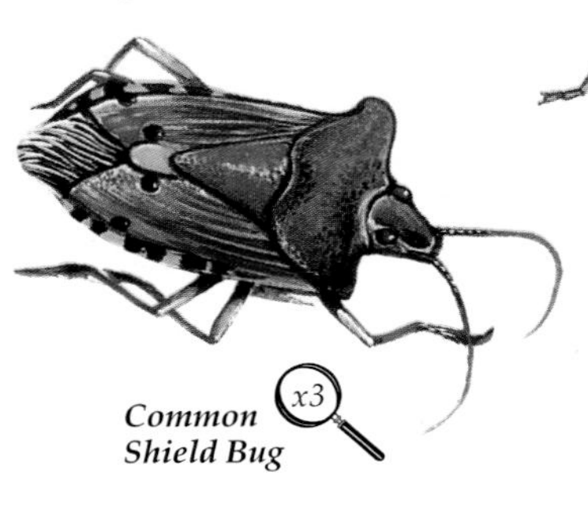

Common Shield Bug x3

Pied Shield Bug

The Common Shield Bug preys on caterpillars and other larvae found on oak and fruit trees.

When her nymphs hatch, the Pied Shield Bug leads them to their food, Dead-Nettle plants.

Stingers and suckers

Both these bugs use their rostrum to pierce the flesh of their prey and suck out nourishing body fluids.

The fierce Heath Assassin Bug x2 preys on other insects.

Bedbugs live in dirty mattresses and drink human blood. x3

Hoppers

All these plant-eating bugs hop away to avoid danger. The Froghoppers are especially athletic, and their nymphs, or young, produce a kind of frothy foam or "cuckoo spit" to hide in.

Nymphs of the Black and Red Froghopper feed on roots underground.

Black and Red Froghopper

The Horned Treehopper lives and feeds on tree branches (especially oak) or in bracken.

Horned Treehopper

The Green Leafhopper feeds on plants in damp meadows and marshes.

Green Leafhopper

The Potato Leafhopper is a pest on potato crops, especially in the USA.

Potato Leafhopper

Common Froghopper

Other plant eaters

Aphids damage plants by drinking the juice, or sap, inside the stem and leaves. The females can produce young without mating.

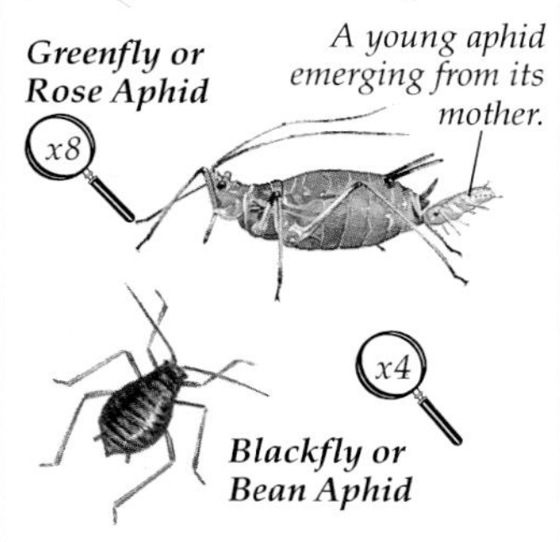

Greenfly or Rose Aphid

A young aphid emerging from its mother.

Blackfly or Bean Aphid

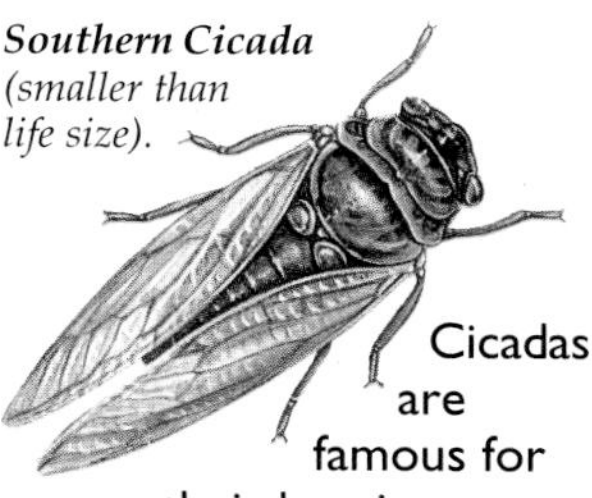

Southern Cicada *(smaller than life size).*

Cicadas are famous for their buzzing sound. They live mainly in warmer climates and drink the sap of ash, pine and olive trees.

A young Froghopper hiding in its own foamy "cuckoo spit".

Water beetles and bugs

Ponds and streams make good habitats for many beetles and bugs. Above and below the surface, food supplies are plentiful, and there are safe hiding places and breeding grounds among the weeds and reeds.

In bright sunshine, groups of Whirligig Beetles come out onto still water surfaces. They can dive for food and fly as well.

Diving beetles...

Underwater divers come to the surface for air, which some store under their wing cases. Many have flattened hind legs, fringed with long hairs, which they use like oars.

Most are fierce predators, feasting on tadpoles, snails, larvae or even small fish.

This beetle is a poor swimmer, but it can fly. It eats mainly water plants.

Water bugs – skimmers

These light, long-legged bugs skate around on the surface of still or slow-moving water. They all feed on other small creatures (alive or dead) attracted to the water.

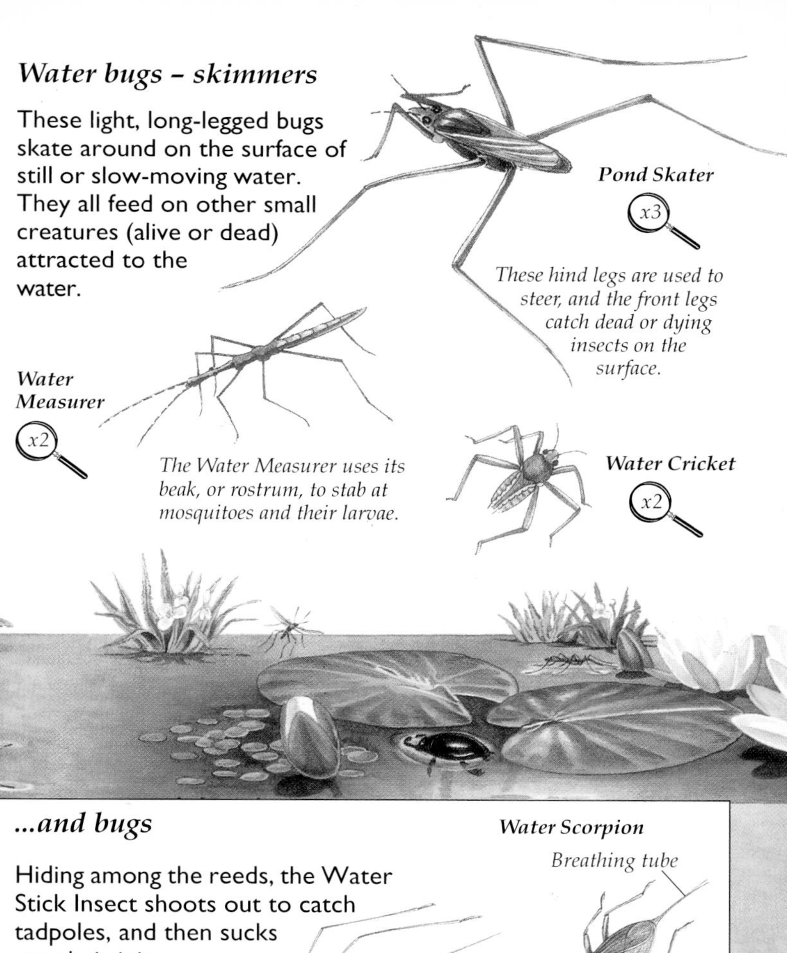

These hind legs are used to steer, and the front legs catch dead or dying insects on the surface.

The Water Measurer uses its beak, or rostrum, to stab at mosquitoes and their larvae.

...and bugs

Hiding among the reeds, the Water Stick Insect shoots out to catch tadpoles, and then sucks out their juices.

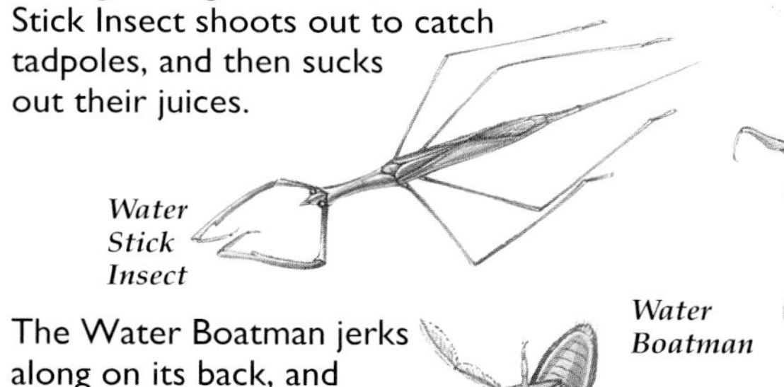

The Water Boatman jerks along on its back, and takes in air at the water surface with its rear end.

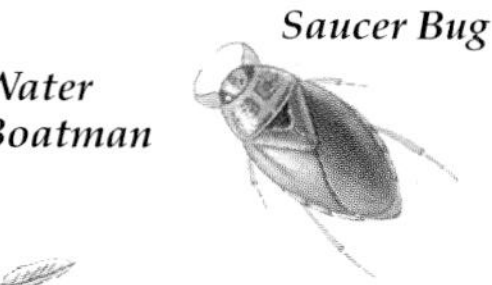

Wasps, bees and ants

Some species of wasps, bees and ants are "social insects". They live in colonies, with a female leader called a queen. All the other members are her children. Other females – called workers – gather food and do all the building work. Males, or drones, live only when they are needed to mate with new queens.

Common Wasp

x4

Wasps

The Common Wasp nests under roofs or underground. Up to 6,000 wasps may live in a colony.

The female Potter Wasp makes a clay pot for each of her larvae, and stocks it with small caterpillars (paralyzed with a sting) for food.

Potter Wasp

The Robin's Pincushion Gall Wasp lives on its own. The female lays eggs in the leaf buds of the wild rose, and the rose grows a mass of threads that looks like a pincushion – called a gall. The larvae grow inside.

Robin's Pincushion Gall Wasp

x2

Gall Wasp larvae develop inside the gall.

Hornet
(shown half size)

Hornets nest in roofs or hollow trees.

Bees

A swarm of Honey Bees

Bumble Bees nest in colonies just underground, sometimes even in old mouseholes. They eat nectar and pollen from flowers.

Bumble Bee

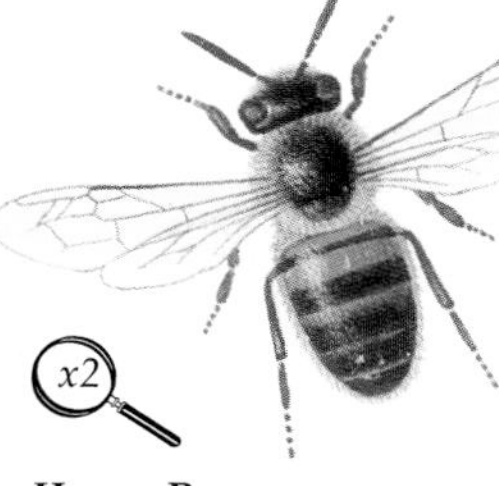

Honey Bee

Honey Bees are social insects. They make honey from flowers' nectar, and store it up during the summer to eat over the winter. Workers produce wax for honeycombs from glands in their abdomens.

The Leaf Cutter Bee lives on its own. The female rolls tubes with pieces cut from rose leaves. She stocks them with nectar and pollen, and lays an egg in each one.

Leaf Cutter Bee

Ants

All ants live in large, social groups and work together. Only the queen and males have wings. Yellow Meadow Ants and Red Ants "farm" aphids in their nests for the sweet liquid they excrete, called honeydew. The Black Ant is the most common in gardens.

Black Ant

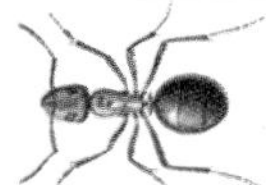

Wood Ant

Yellow Meadow Ant

Red Ant

All these species are between 3-10mm (up to ½ in) long.

Singers, springers...

In sunny weather, male crickets and grasshoppers make a singing noise with their wings or back legs to attract females. Crickets have long antennae, whereas grasshoppers' are short. Both groups use their strong back legs to leap, and then glide with open wings.

Speckled Bush Cricket

The male Speckled Bush Cricket sings with a high-pitched chirp. The female responds in song too.

The House Cricket is often found in heated buildings, greenhouses, and rubbish tips. It has a shrill song.

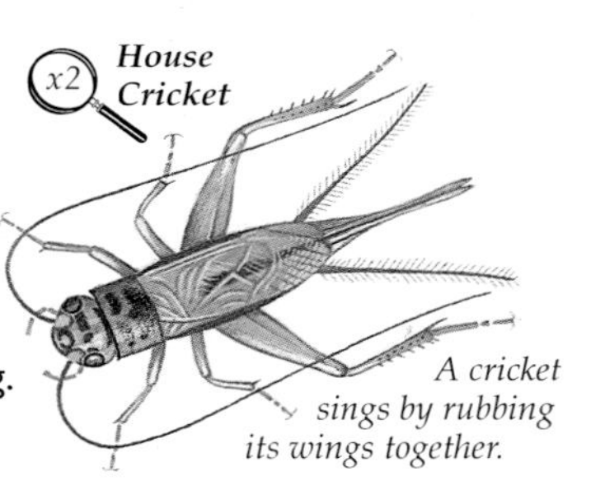

House Cricket (x2)

A cricket sings by rubbing its wings together.

Oak Bush Crickets leap around low shrubs. Instead of singing, the male summons a mate by drumming his back feet on a leaf.

Oak Bush Cricket

The hissing song of the Common Green Grasshopper sounds a little like a moped approaching.

Common Green Grasshopper (x2)

Large Marsh Grasshopper (x2)

The Large Marsh Grasshopper lives in damp places like bogs and swamps. The male makes a soft, slow ticking song.

Grasshoppers rub their back legs against their wings to make a noise.

...and lurkers

Stick Insects lurk camouflaged in bushes in wamer climates. They eat plant material.

Stick Insect
(shown smaller than life-size)

Common Earwig

x2

An earwig spreads and raises pincers when it is threatened.

Earwigs eat small insects, usually dead, as well as leaves and fruits. Females guard the nymphs until they can look after themselves.

You might see wingless Silverfish in your home, on walls or in damp, dark corners in the kitchen or bathroom.

x2

Silverfish

Cockroaches scuttle around warm buildings all through the year. They can eat almost anything, from humans' food to books, leather or photographic film. They leave foul-smelling droppings.

Common Cockroach

The Praying Mantis waits for its insect prey in scrub and tall grass. The female sometimes eats the male while they are mating. It is found in warmer climates in Southern Europe and US.

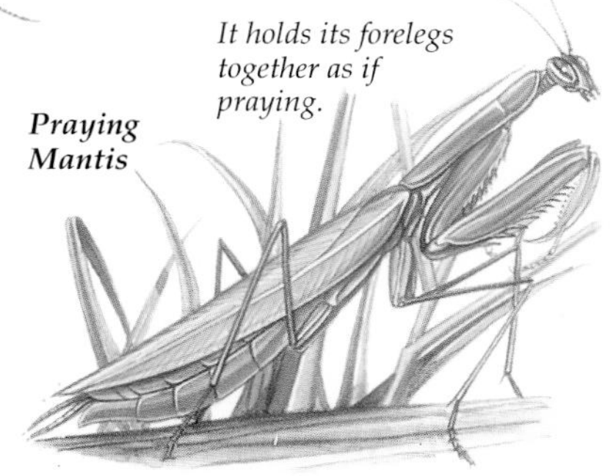

Praying Mantis

It holds its forelegs together as if praying.

Flies

Flies have only one pair of wings. All flies feed on liquids. Some suck flowers' nectar, or sting animals to drink their blood. Others vomit onto their food, and then stamp around to soften the food into liquid form.

Bluebottle Fly (*same size as Greenbottle*)

Its loud hum warns you when the Horse Fly is near. The female sucks human blood. It is found mainly in old forests.

Horse Fly

Greenbottle Fly (x2)

Both Greenbottles and Bluebottles lay eggs on dead animal flesh. This way their legless larvae, or maggots, have food ready when they hatch.

The Hover Fly hovers by flowers to suck nectar. Its markings mimic a wasp for protection.

(x2) *Hover Fly*

Robber Fly

A Robber Fly killing a Damselfly (x2)

The fast-flying Robber Fly pounces on other insects in the air and sucks them dry.

The Dung Fly (left) lays its eggs in fresh cowpats, so its larvae can eat the dung. The adult preys on other flies.

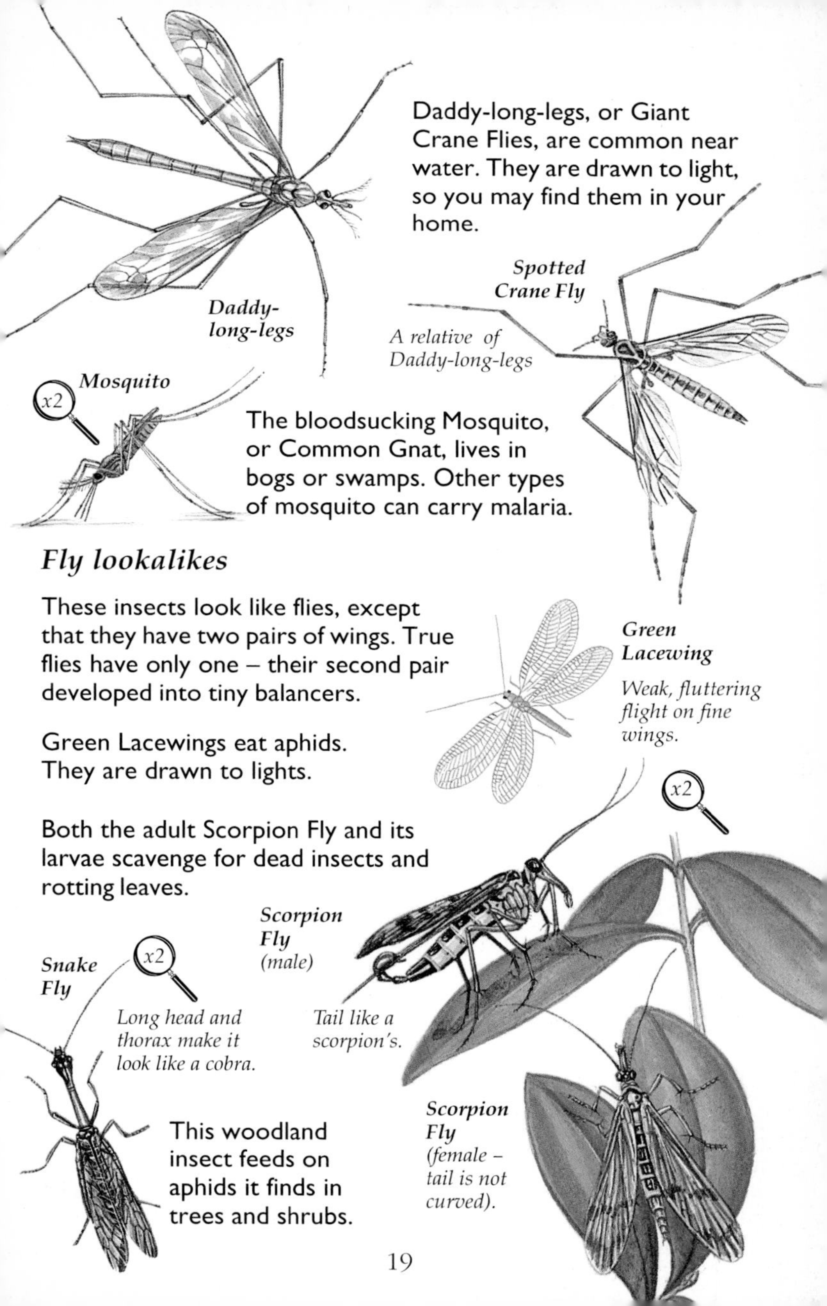

Daddy-long-legs, or Giant Crane Flies, are common near water. They are drawn to light, so you may find them in your home.

The bloodsucking Mosquito, or Common Gnat, lives in bogs or swamps. Other types of mosquito can carry malaria.

Fly lookalikes

These insects look like flies, except that they have two pairs of wings. True flies have only one – their second pair developed into tiny balancers.

Green Lacewings eat aphids. They are drawn to lights.

Both the adult Scorpion Fly and its larvae scavenge for dead insects and rotting leaves.

This woodland insect feeds on aphids it finds in trees and shrubs.

Larvae and nymphs

Insects go through different stages before they become adults (see page 5). The next three pages will help you identify some larvae and nymphs, and the adults they will grow into.

Maggots and grubs

All these wrigglers are the larvae of different insects. Where they live depends on the shape of their body – and whether or not they have legs.

The Birch Sawfly larva has nine pairs of legs. It crawls around feeding on birch leaves in late summer.

Birch Sawfly larva *x5*

Birch Sawfly *(half size)*

The House Fly lays eggs on decaying flesh or food so that the legless maggots hatch right on their food.

House Fly

x3 ***House Fly maggot***

Bluebottle and Greenbottle larvae are similar to this.

Cockchafer larvae feed on plant roots, so the adult lays her eggs in the soil.

Cockchafer Beetle *(half size)*

Cockchafer larva

Telescopic maggot

The Rat-tailed Maggot (larva of the Drone Fly) lives in mud in stagnant ponds. It breathes through a telescopic tube which it extends to reach the water surface.

Drone Fly

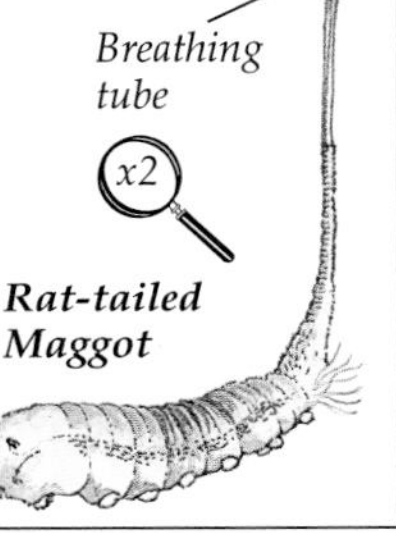

Rat-tailed Maggot

Underwater nursery

Many insects start their life underwater, breathing through gills, even if they will turn into airborne adults like Dragonflies or Mayflies.

The Mayfly nymph lives in the water for up to three years. But it lives for only a few hours after becoming an adult Mayfly.

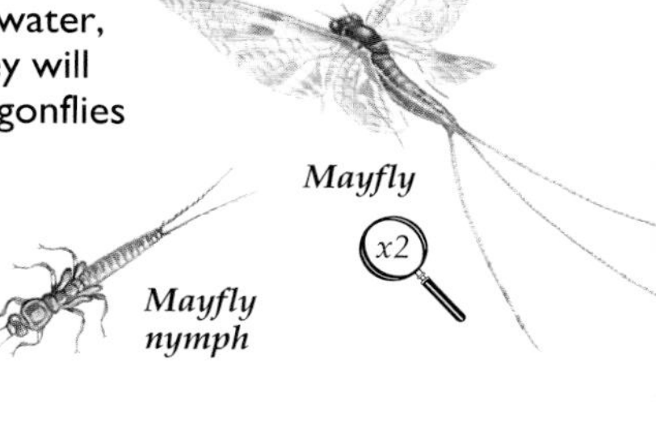

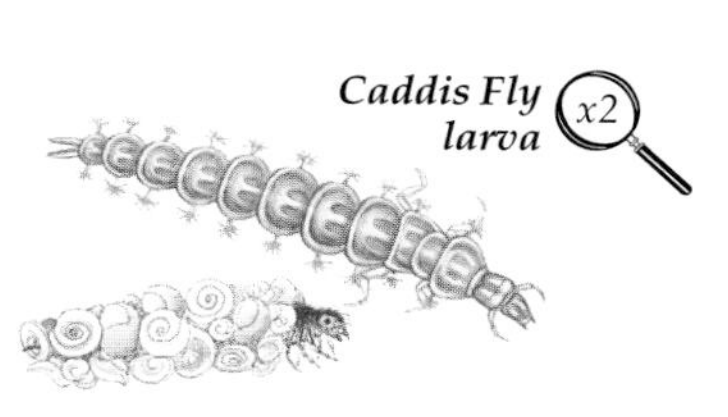

A Caddis Fly larva crawls around the pond bed in this protective case.

The Caddis Fly's plant-eating larva makes its own protective case of shells, stones and leaves.

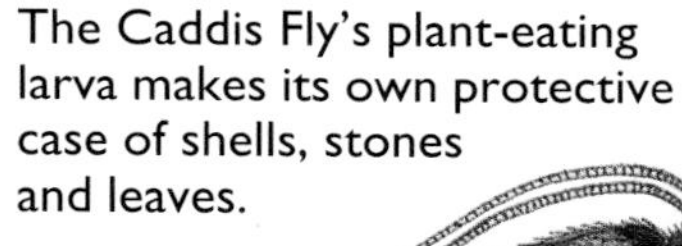

Dragonfly

The adult Dragonfly lives only for about a month.

The Dragonfly nymph is a fierce underwater predator. After about four years, in the summer, the nymph crawls out of the water. Its skin splits and the adult Dragonfly emerges.

A Dragonfly stays near water to prey on other creatures.

Old skin of Dragonfly nymph left behind.

An adult Dragonfly emerging from the nymph's skin. Its body hardens and its new wings expand.

Caterpillars

Caterpillars are larvae of butterflies and moths. They make a juicy snack for birds and other predators, so many have evolved protective weapons or disguises.

Hairy caterpillars

These hairy caterpillars (often called "woolly bears") are hard for predators to swallow. The hairs can cause a rash on human skin.

Garden Tiger Moth caterpillar
(half life-size)

Dense tufts or tussocks of hairs

Vapourer Moth caterpillar

Warnings and camouflage

Insects that are red, yellow, orange and black warn that they taste foul. Others have scary markings or use camouflage for protection.

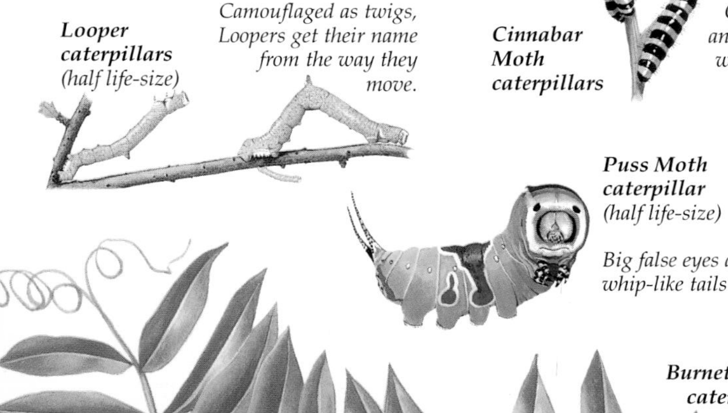

Looper caterpillars
(half life-size)

Camouflaged as twigs, Loopers get their name from the way they move.

Cinnabar Moth caterpillars

Orange and black warning stripes

Puss Moth caterpillar
(half life-size)

Big false eyes and whip-like tails

Burnet Moth caterpillar

Warning markings

Legs and segments

Millipedes and centipedes have more legs than other creepy crawlies. Their bodies are divided into lots of rings or segments.

Segments

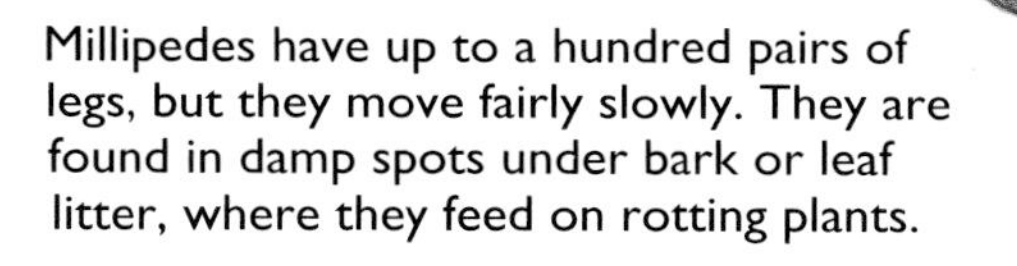

Millipedes have up to a hundred pairs of legs, but they move fairly slowly. They are found in damp spots under bark or leaf litter, where they feed on rotting plants.

Millipedes curl up if they are disturbed.

x2 ***Millipede***

Its long body has a more rounded shape than a centipede's.

The Pill Millipede (right) looks like a woodlouse but it has more legs – 17 to 19 pairs.

It can curl up into a tight ball.

A centipede is a fast-moving carnivore. It uses a pair of poison claws at its head to kill small insects and worms. It is found under leaf litter, stones or in soil.

x2 ***Centipede***

Around thirty legs

Flat body

x4 ***Woodlouse***

Woodlice

Woodlice are land-based relatives of crabs and lobsters. They live in damp, dark places, beneath stones or rotting logs, and feed on dead plants.

x4 ***Pill Bug***

A Pill Bug is related to woodlice. It can roll into a ball when disturbed.

Spiders

All spiders are carnivores (meat-eaters). Some spin silk webs to catch insects or other tiny animals. Others hunt by night or lie in wait for food instead.

Garden Spider's circular web, called an orb web

Spiders are not insects. They have eight legs, and their bodies have two parts, rather than three.

The Garden Spider hangs head down in the middle of its large orb web. The sticky threads catch passing creatures.

Garden Spider *x2*

House Spiders spin triangular webs, called cobwebs, in corners. Insects get their feet trapped in the dense mat of threads.

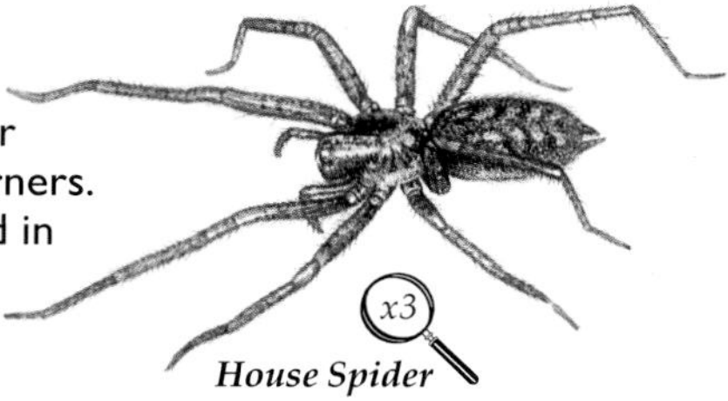

House Spider *x3*

Wall Spider

Wall Spiders spin web tubes in cracks in walls. A tripwire alerts the spider when any prey comes near.

Hunting Spiders live in a funnel in the middle of a large greyish web. They also hunt for food in open woodland.

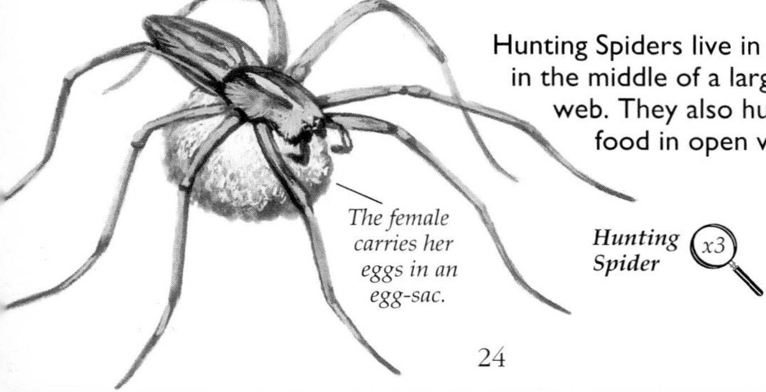

The female carries her eggs in an egg-sac.

Hunting Spider *x3*

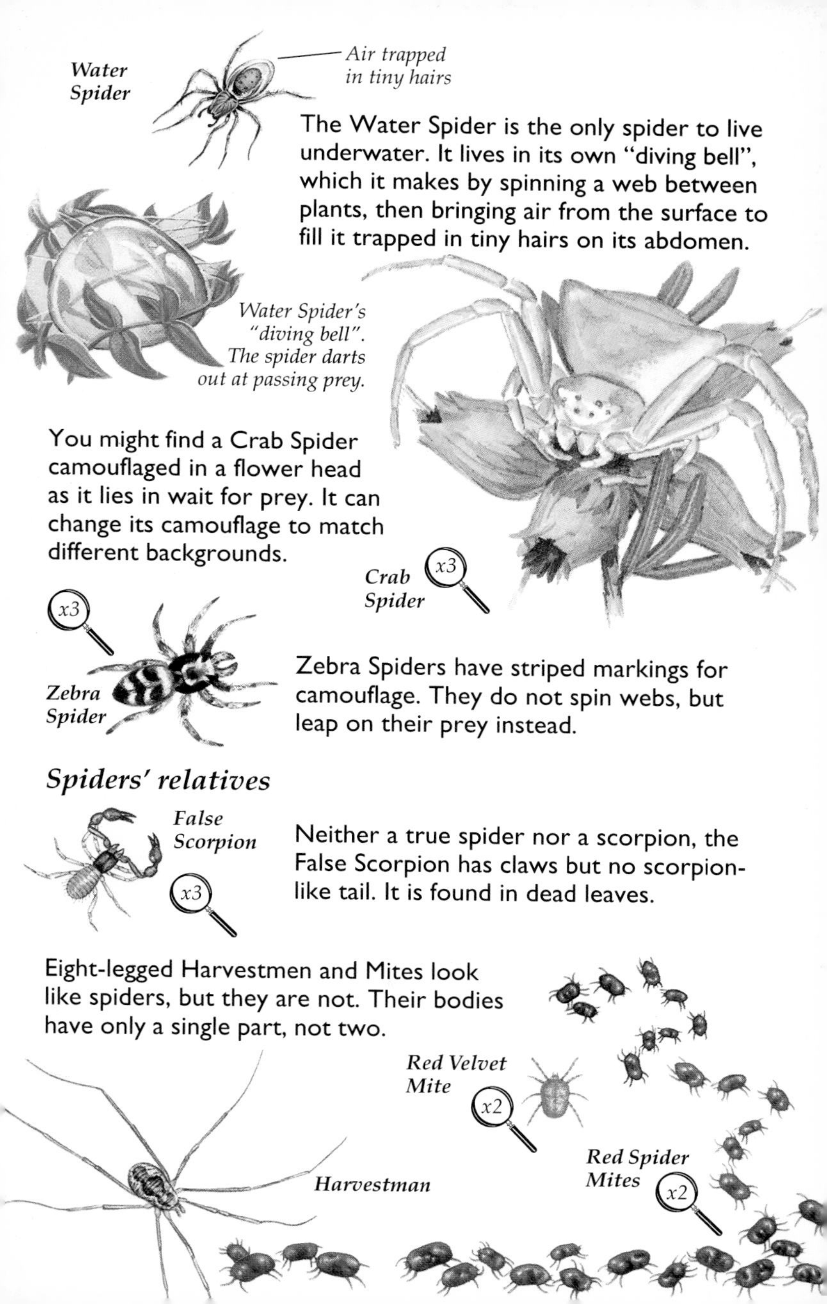

The Water Spider is the only spider to live underwater. It lives in its own "diving bell", which it makes by spinning a web between plants, then bringing air from the surface to fill it trapped in tiny hairs on its abdomen.

You might find a Crab Spider camouflaged in a flower head as it lies in wait for prey. It can change its camouflage to match different backgrounds.

Zebra Spiders have striped markings for camouflage. They do not spin webs, but leap on their prey instead.

Spiders' relatives

Neither a true spider nor a scorpion, the False Scorpion has claws but no scorpion-like tail. It is found in dead leaves.

Eight-legged Harvestmen and Mites look like spiders, but they are not. Their bodies have only a single part, not two.

Snails, slugs and worms

Snails and slugs are gastropods, which means "stomach-foot". The flat body acts as a foot, and a snail or slug moves by waves of muscle movement passing along it. Its slimy mucus trail guides it back to regular feeding spots, where it eats leaves and rotting plants.

Banded Snail

Eye at the tip of each long antenna

Tongue has rows of tiny teeth (like a cheese grater), for filing off food.

x2

Snails

In winter or in dry weather, a snail retreats into its shell and seals the opening with layers of mucus, which hardens as it dries.

Garden Snail

The Garden Snail is a common garden pest, eating vegetables and plant leaves.

Strawberry Snail

The Strawberry Snail has a sandy or purplish-brown shell. It prefers damp conditions.

Pointed Snails live on grassy banks or sand dunes.

Pointed Snail

Great Ramshorn Snail

x2

This snail lives in water, including very stagnant ponds. It eats algae and rotting material on the mud at the bottom.

Slugs

Slugs are simply snails without shells. In cold and dry weather they burrow deep into the soil. Their mucus tastes unpleasant, which protects them from predators.

Garden Slug

A slug's slime is so thick and protective that it can climb over a very sharp knife unharmed.

Large Black Slug

It has grooves along its back.

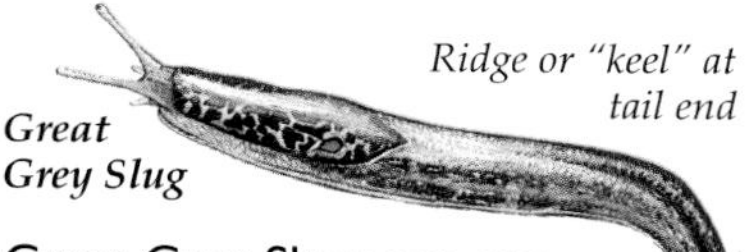

Ridge or "keel" at tail end

Great Grey Slug

Great Grey Slugs can grow as long as 20cm (8in).

The Large Black Slug lives in damp grass and heaths. It can also be grey, brown or orange, and grows up to 15cm (6in) long.

Worms

All the creatures below belong to the worm family, called annelids. Their bodies are made up of rings or segments.

The Horse Leech swims in ponds and ditches. It feeds by sucking the blood of fish or frogs. Despite its name, it does not suck the blood of horses (or humans).

Horse Leech (about half life-size)

Wormcast on sand

Lugworm in burrow

Lugworms live in U-shaped burrows in the sand. They suck in sand and digest any edible particles. They grow up to 15cm (6in) long.

Earthworms swallow soil as they burrow, and digest any edible matter. They can grow up to 30cm (12in) long. Each worm has both male and female organs.

Common Earthworm

Scorecard

All the creepy crawlies shown in this book are listed here, in alphabetical order. When you spot one, fill in the date next to its name. Rare creatures score more points than common ones.

	Score	*Date seen*
Banded Snail	5	
Bedbug	25	
Bee Beetle	20	
Birch Sawfly	10	
Birch Sawfly larva	10	
Black Ant	5	
Blackfly	5	
Bluebottle Fly	5	
Bombadier Beetle	15	
Bumble Bee	5	
Burnet Moth caterpillar	10	
Burying Beetle, Red and Black	10	
Caddis Fly	10	
Caddis Fly larva	10	
Centipede	5	
Cicada	25	
Cinnabar Moth caterpillar	10	
Click Beetle	15	
Cockchafer Beetle	10	
Cockchafer larva	10	
Cockroach	5	
Colorado Beetle	25	
Crab Spider	10	
"cuckoo spit"	5	
Daddy-long-legs	5	
Devil's Coach Horse Beetle	5	
Dragonfly	10	
Dragonfly nymph	10	
Drone Fly	10	
Dung Fly	5	

	Score	*Date seen*
Earthworm	5	
Earwig	5	
False Scorpion	10	
Firefly (US only)	15	
Froghopper, Black and Red	10	
Froghopper, Common	5	
Garden Slug	5	
Garden Snail	5	
Garden Spider	5	
Glow-worm (Europe only)	20	
Great Diving Beetle	10	
Great Grey Slug	20	
Great Ramshorn Snail	10	
Great Silver Water Beetle	20	
Greenbottle Fly	5	
Greenfly	5	
Green Grasshopper, Common	10	
Green Lacewing	5	
Green Leafhopper	10	
Green Shield Bug	10	
Green Tiger Beetle	10	
Green Tortoise Beetle	10	
Harvestman	5	
Hawthorn Shield Bug	10	
Heath Assassin Bug	10	
Hercules Beetle (US only)	25	
Honey Bee	5	
Horned Treehopper	15	
Hornet	20	
Horse Fly	10	

	Score	Date seen
Horse Leech	15	
House Cricket	15	
House Fly	5	
House Fly maggot	5	
House Spider	5	
Hover Fly	5	
Hunting Spider	15	
Ladybird, Eyed	20	
Ladybird, Two Spot	5	
Ladybird, Seven Spot	5	
Ladybird, 14 Spot	15	
Ladybird, 22 Spot	15	
Large Black Slug	10	
Large Marsh Grasshopper	20	
Leaf Cutter Bee	15	
Looper caterpillar	5	
Lugworm cast	5	
Mayfly	10	
Mayfly nymph	10	
Millipede	10	
Mosquito	5	
Nut Weevil	15	
Oak Bush Cricket	10	
Pied Shield Bug	10	
Pill Bug	10	
Pill Millipede	10	
Pointed Snail	5	
Pond Skater	5	
Potato Leafhopper	10	
Potter Wasp	15	
Praying Mantis	25	
Puss Moth caterpillar	15	
Rat-tailed Maggot	10	

	Score	Date seen
Red Ant	5	
Red Spider Mite	10	
Red Velvet Mite	10	
Robber Fly	15	
Robin's Pincushion Gall	10	
Saucer Bug	10	
Scarlet-tipped Flower Beetle	10	
Scorpion Fly	10	
Shield Bug, Common	10	
Silverfish	10	
Snake Fly	15	
Speckled Bush Cricket	10	
Spotted Crane Fly	20	
Stag Beetle	15	
Strawberry Snail	10	
Stick Insect	25	
Tiger Moth caterpillar	5	
Vapourer Moth caterpillar	5	
Wall Spider	10	
Wasp Beetle	10	
Wasp, Common	5	
Water Boatman	10	
Water Cricket	25	
Water Measurer	10	
Water Scorpion	10	
Water Spider	15	
Water Stick Insect	15	
Whirligig Beetle	10	
Wood Ant	10	
Woodlouse	5	
Yellow Meadow Ant	5	
Zebra Spider	5	

Glossary

Below are explanations of some important words used in this book. Words printed in **bold** type within a definition have their own separate entry.

abdomen The hind part of an **insect** or other creepy crawly, behind the legs.

alga (plural: algae) A simple plant that usually grows in water.

antenna (plural: antennae) A sensitive feeler used, for example, for smelling. In some **species** (like land snails), one pair of antennae bears the eyes.

camouflage Markings which help an animal to remain hidden against its background.

carnivore An animal which feeds on other animals.

chrysalis The **pupa** of a butterfly.

colony A group of **social insects** which live and work together, such as ants and some bees and wasps.

drone Male **social insect**, which lives only at certain times of year, when it is needed to mate with the **queen**.

elytra (singular: elytron) The hard, protective wing cases of **insects** like beetles. The elytra developed from the front pair of wings.

excrete To get rid of waste from the body.

gall A swelling on a plant caused by **insect larvae** feeding on the plant's tissue.

hibernate To spend the winter in a sleepy, inactive state.

honeydew The sweet liquid **excreted** by some **insects** (such as aphids) and eaten by others (such as ants).

insect The biggest group of species of **invertebrate**, each with six legs and a three-part body (head, **thorax** and **abdomen**).

invertebrate An animal without a backbone.

larva (plural: larvae) An **insect** at the stage in between egg and **pupa**.

mimicry The use of markings or shape which copy another (often fierce) **species**, to help fend off **predators**.

moult The shedding of skin to allow growth.

mucus The slimy liquid that snails and slugs leave as a trail.

nectar A sweet-tasting liquid produced by flowers. Many insects feed on nectar.

nymph The young form of an insect that does not pass through the stage of being a **pupa**. It is a smaller, wingless form of the adult.

predator An animal that kills and eats other animals.

prey An animal hunted by a **predator**.

pupa An **insect** in the stage between being a **larva** and maturing into an adult.

queen The female head of a **colony** of **social insects**. Only the queen lays eggs.

rostrum The long, tube-like, stabbing mouthpart of bugs, or the extended head of a group of beetles called weevils.

scavenger An animal that feeds on dead flesh or rotting plants.

segment A ring or section of the body of animals like worms or woodlice.

social insects Insects (such as ants) that live in a **colony** and are organized into three groups (the **queen**, **workers** and **drones**) which each have different duties.

species A group of animals with the same characteristics that can breed together.

thorax The part of the body between the head and abdomen. In **insects** the thorax bears all the legs, and wings if any.

worker A female **social insect** who cannot breed. These insects work for the **colony**.

Additional illustrations by

Joyce Bee, Stephen Bennett, Rowland Berry, Michelle Emblem, Don Forrest, John Francis, William Giles, Victoria Goaman, Rebecca Hardy, Tim Hayward, Chris Howell-Jones, Christine Howes, Roger Kent, Jonathan Langley, Richard Lewington, Mick Loates, Alan Male, Annabel Milne, Dee Morgan, Robert Morton, Richard Orr, David Palmer, Julie Piper, Gillian Platt, Barry Raynor, Philip Richardson, Jim Robins, Peter Stebbing, David Watson, Adrian Williams, Roy Wiltshire, John Yates.

This book is based on material previously published in Usborne Spotter's Guides: *Insects*, *Woodland Life* and *Ponds and Lakes*, Usborne Nature Trail Books: *Insect Watching*, *Garden Wildlife* and *Ponds and Streams*, Usborne First Nature: *Creepy Crawlies* and *Butterflies and Moths*, *Usborne Mysteries and Marvels of Nature*, and *The Usborne Illustrated Encyclopedia: The Natural World*.

Index

First published in 1996 by Usborne Publishing Ltd, Usborne House, 83-85 Saffron Hill, London EC1N 8RT, England.

Printed in Italy.